BEYOND THE IRON GATE

A PENNIES WORTH OF DREAD NOVELLA

M.A. BROWN

To anyone who has had to endure in
silence.

Contents

The moon was a woman curled in the sky. Though the story varied on why it was there that she chose to reside in a silver cocoon of her hair. Some say it was a curse that put her there, a curse by the very same witches who spelled the fence. Some say she was the sacrifice they made, a barter with the gods to give them the power to imbue the fence with the magic to keep away the beasts. But my favorite version goes like this:

There was once a young maiden born with hair as white as the driven snow, eyes as clear as glass, and skin as pale as skimmed milk. She was rare in her beauty but even rarer in her kindness, and all who knew her loved her, but none more so than the man who lived in the woods. He was tender like moss and smelled of woodsmoke and green things and would leave for her flowers on the sill of her window. She grew to love him and would look for him in between the trees. But the girl who would become the moon was born of wealth, and her father would never consent to a marriage to a woodsman, and any attempt she made to beseech him fell on deaf ears.

My mother and I lived on the farthest edge of town where the air was heavy with the tang of old iron and abandoned hopes. My garden backed right up to the fence that kept the evils of the world at bay, where it leeched rust into the snow, tingeing it a bloody orange. The bare black branches of the woods beyond, silhouetted in the slender moonlight, looked like the desperate hands of the damned trying to claw their way out of the underworld. Or perhaps they were just trying to get away from the beasts that supposedly lived within their shadows.

The midnight wind whispered its secrets through the trees and sent fingers of fog slipping through the wrought bars of the fence to grab at my too-skinny ankles and tease at the hem of my woolen skirts. I knew better than to be out past curfew, but the Huntsmen didn't often patrol this side of the fence, not even when the moon was full. And as for the beasts, well, I wasn't nearly as afraid of them as I ought to be. Besides, hunger gnawed too incessantly at my rib bones to allow me restful sleep.

I bent to brush the kiss of frost from my shrubs, the winter berries on them just barely plump enough to pluck, when an errant thorn bit into the soft, vulnerable flesh between my sleeve and my cuff. I hissed, bit off a curse, and yanked my glove from my hand before the beading blood could stain its edges. I held my wrist up, exposing it to a shaft of icy moonlight to better see the tear when betwixt my pale fingers I spied two golden eyes blooming in the puddled darkness beyond the fence.

Everything stilled—my heart, the air around me, even the trees seemed to hold their breaths—as the eyes drifted closer to the peeling metal bars. A burgeoning droplet of blood welled up and plunged from my wrist, its collision with the frigid ground audible against the silence of the night. I gasped, and my eyes darted between the looming creature that stalked toward the boundary fence and the single burgundy drop on the white snow. My heart began to pound, begging me to run like the prey I was for the safety of a locked door. But morbid curiosity rooted my feet to the ground.

A slow silver smile was the first feature to come into focus, as if the watching moon wanted to make sure I saw just how sharp his teeth were before I got a look at the rest of him. But the rest of him . . . the rest of him distracted me from that more predatory feature. He stood nearly as tall as the fence itself, which was as tall as nearly two men, and made the whole thing seem utterly useless in that moment, no more of a defense against the wicked things of the world than a child's favorite blanket drawn over their head.

He looked more man than beast, with a crop of dark-brown hair, spun through with golden strands to match his molten, gilded eyes, a few shades lighter than my own, which blended with the snow-churned muddied ground, and tawny skin that spoke of days spent in the sun that I didn't know even touched the depths of the wood. He dressed like a common man, though he was not dressed for the season; it was as though winter's bite feared him as much as us mere mortals.

"You're bleeding, Little Wolf." His words were a low growl that swirled on fogged breath through the air to brush against my cheek in a sinful caress.

"I'm no wolf," I whispered, before biting my lip on a sharp inhale. I hadn't meant to speak those words aloud. I hadn't meant to speak at all. There were rhymes taught to children from the cradle to remind them to stay away from the fence and what to do should they ever come across a monster. But in that moment, the echoing thread of them was too thin in the back of my memories for me to grasp.

He prowled closer, his steps eerily silent, and wrapped his claw-tipped fingers around the bars. He cocked his head to the side, and said, "Are you sure about that?"

His gaze bored into me as if he could read all the broken wishes I had scrawled onto my soul in blood. My breath hitched on my ribs as his eyes trailed down my neck, across my collarbone, to the crook of my elbow, before landing on the crimson slash across my wrist. I felt the gaze like the gentle scrape of a knife.

The corner of his lips curled. "I could fix your hurt for you, Little Wolf. If you just slip your arm on through." He tapped his claw along the vermilion-crusted bars, and the echo reverberated in a rusty shudder down the row of iron.

My lips parted, swollen from biting them shut. I'd intended to tell him no, to go away. I'd meant once again to obey my heart, to turn and run, but as though hypnotized by the tenor of his voice and the fire in his gilded eyes, I simply whispered, "Please, don't eat me," before I took a lethal step forward and slipped my wrist through the gap that was just shy of the width of a man's head.

My ribs ached as my heart tried to run away with itself. His hand left the bars and gently curled around the back of mine, and his eyebrow lifted as he drew my hand closer to his face. "Something tells me, Little Wolf, that you wouldn't mind being devoured half as much as you think you would." His words were tinted with something potent—like a promise.

He bent his head, keeping his eyes locked on mine as he drew his tongue along the scrape. Gooseflesh erupted up my arm, spreading to envelop my whole body, coaxing out a whimper from between my parted lips. I yanked my arm back and gasped. The wound was gone, and the skin was knitted back together. I stared in amazement between the bars, my throat working to find words through the befuddled fog of stark amazement. How in the gods' names was such a thing even possible?

"I think the words you're looking for, Little Wolf, are thank you." He smirked, leaning a corded forearm against the fence and resting his forehead indolently upon it.

"Rosewynn," I whispered, "my name is Rosewynn, not Little Wolf."

He reached his free hand through the gap and brushed an errant strand of ash-brown hair off my face, tucking it behind my ear. His hand lingered for a breath as though he thought to press it to my cheek tenderly, or maybe he wanted to wrap it around my throat and squeeze the life from my lungs. Each seemed as likely as the other.

"You shouldn't give your name so freely to monsters in the dark."

The slam of a shutter behind me ripped my attention from his entrancing face. I whipped my head around, and the hair he'd so carefully tucked behind my ear flew out of place, caught in the same breeze that fiddled with the loose board. When I turned back, the beast was gone, leaving not even a footprint in the snow to mark his passing presence.

My erratic pulse never wavered as I hiked my skirts and followed the foot path back to the cottage. I peered over my shoulder only twice before climbing back into my window, my hunger forgotten. I didn't know what I hoped to see more of: nothing but the endless dark or twin yellow eyes cutting through the gloom.

I dreamed of those eyes upon me through the night, and when I rose in the morning and peered out the window through the curling mist, I found a bouquet of beasts-bane flowers tied to the fence with an emerald ribbon.

Before donning my worn gray cloak and drawing up my cowl over my black dress, I braided the purple bruise-colored bell-shaped flowers through my hair and tied the end with the ribbon to brighten my dour and drab, sleepless appearance. Besides, I liked the reminder of him, the reminder that it, that *he* had not been just a dream.

Mother still slept in her chair by the hearth, her chest rising and falling spasmodically. She'd come down with fever some weeks back, and though the burning passed, it left her lungs ravaged. Her rattling breaths were an ever-present dirge lilting through our home. Vile though they were, they were reassuring. At least she still lived. Were she to die, I would be cast out of my home. Only men or widows could own property in our village, and a home, even one as careworn and close to the fence as ours, was coveted. I'd seen lurkers along the usually desolate path that wound like unspooled thread through our patch of sparse woods, necks craned as though they could see whether or not death lurked on our stoop ready to snatch my mother away.

I gathered the bucket from its spot on the counter and spun to find mother's glassy, dew-filled eyes on me. "Where are you going?" she croaked. The words rasped over her parched and cracked lips. I hitched the frayed rope handle of the bucket up into the crook of my elbow.

"To the well, Mother, I'll be back soon." I turned again to go when her words snagged the hem of my skirt like a clawed fist.

"You were out in the night again. By the fence." I didn't look at her. I kept my gaze nailed to the wood-planked door where flowers were once painted, bright purple beasts-bane bells like the ones in my hair and blue milk thistles. My father had painted them there as a gift to my mother, and now the flowers were little more than flecks of paint, and my father was little more than worm fodder in the soil. "You of all people, Rosewynn, need to stay away from those bars. How many times must I tell you?"

"At least one more time, Mother," I answered, but the words were softly spoken and swept away by the bitter winter wind wriggling itself through the gap between door and frame as I slipped through.

Outside the gales blew with vigor, churning the placid gray clouds into a temperamental black tempest that threatened to unleash itself on those of us unfortunate enough to live in its wake. Even the birds seemed too wary of it to be out singing their usual mournful melodies.

The slurry of snow and mud along the path had my cracked leather boots soaked and sodden before the first weathered stone building of our nearest neighbor came into view. The Larkins' farm, if such a pittance of land could be called such. I'd once entertained notions of marrying their eldest son, but such fancies were quickly squashed when I realized the reputation my mother had had by association ruined my reputation before I'd had a chance to grow up and garner my own.

I toed a rock out of my way with a sigh that bordered on wistful. Even if she were to pass, and some families were to feel charitable toward me, I was too old now to be considered, by most, useful as a wife. Which seemed laughable considering I'd only seen eight and twenty years. Men wanted fresh fruit, my mother always reminded me, not a piece that had been plucked and set upon the shelf to shrivel and molder.

The path widened, opening onto where the gray stone buildings of town stood in somber rows like a mouthful of rotted teeth, their roofs bent and huddled against the icy wind. I picked my way warily down the uneven cobbled-stone road, careful to avoid eye contact. I kept my head down and my hood up, moving quickly but not too quickly so as not to draw any unnecessary attention. Though fortunately, there were few about at this hour, and those who were skirted out of my path. A call for alms turned my head, and a boy no more than ten, his face gaunt and his voice weak with hunger, cried out from a cowl that had seen better days, and I veered slightly in his direction, just long enough to empty my pocket of dried winter berries into his bowl and move on before he could spurn the hand that fed him. And I silently prayed he would accept the offering and not empty it on the street, fearing it cursed.

The well squatted in the center of the town's square, its wide mouth screaming at the sky as we slow-ly bled it dry. Once upon a time, there had been several wells scattered throughout the sanctuary of the fence, but they'd long since been declared tainted or dried up by the Huntsmen's council and bricked over. Across the vacant square, the solitary gate stood sentry, twisted and tangled. The properties of the enchanted iron kept the beasts of the woods at bay; though as I witnessed last night, perhaps it didn't work as well as everyone believed. My stomach felt peculiar at the thought, as though it were filled with a riotous murder of crows eager to take flight.

I set my bucket down on the iced-over stones, careful not to lose my footing as I leaned forward to grab the well's rope. The pulley's creaking echoed shrilly, rankling my nerves and setting my already-near-chattering teeth on edge. The bucket below landed in the dark water with a splash. I jiggled the rope, allowing the bucket to tip and drink its fill before I began the arduous task of dredging it back up again.

Leaning forward over the cracked stone lip of the well, I hooked a gloved finger over the rim of the bucket and tugged it toward where I stood, wary not to jostle it too much lest I spill.

"Well, well, what do we have here?" a voice sliced through the cold with the sharpness of a headsman's axe.

I startled, my spine going ridged, just as I bent to pour the water from the well's bucket into my own. I lost a quarter of its contents on my skirt as punishment for my lapse in vigilance. I'd managed to avoid Yorick for the past two moon cycles, but as the dark gods would have it, my luck—meager as it was—had finally run dry.

I stood and leaned to drop the well bucket back into place, studiously keeping my eyes off Yorick. He was a Huntsman, all thick muscles and eyes gleaming with devious intent, as marked by the silver axe badge embroidered on the chest of his forest-green cloak.

Huntsmen were meant to be the protectors of our people, guarding the rare trade wagons through the forest, patrolling the gate and the fence, and killing any beasts that sought to get too close to our homes. They had a codex, which they lived by, though as the beloved son of the Head Huntsman, Yorick saw himself above such trivial moralities. He'd also lived a comfortable existence, afforded privileges the rest of us had not. Anything he'd wanted, he'd been given, felt entitled to. But that entitlement wasn't purely limited to goods and food, it extended to flesh, and he'd inexplicably decided he wanted mine. Perhaps it was the forbidden nature of my being—I was the untouchable pariah he wasn't supposed to want, thus making me rare and valuable. I'd never bothered to ask. I didn't want to know. I didn't want him.

"Don't be rude, Rosewynn." His voice slid like rancid oil across my skin. There was something about the way my name rolled off his tongue that made me feel dirty. "Say something. Ask me how I've been." He raked a hand over his short, cropped mud-brown hair, a tick he had that I'd long ago learned boded ill.

I cleared my throat, thickly coated and strangled with nerves, and folded my damp, gloved hands across my ribs, bracing myself. His words were always games, ones I endlessly felt I didn't know the rules to. "Are you hale and well, Yorick?" I asked.

He stepped closer, his breath reeking of stale ale and arrogance as he reached out and shoved the hood of my cloak back and began plucking at the end of my braid, knotted in the green ribbon, where it lay draped over my the swell of my bosom. "These are pretty." He fingered the beasts-bane buds. "Did you get all dressed up for me? Does this mean you're finally going to accept my proposal?"

Burning indignation festered. I was not his to touch, but I kept my tone level and untainted by my emotions. He liked to see my emotions get the best of me. "I am still considering your offer and have yet to arrive at a decision."

Yorick's lips pulled back in a yellowed-tooth snarl as he wrapped my plaited hair around his tight fingered fist, the echo of crumpled petals sharp in my ear. "What exactly is there to consider? It's not like you have suitors lining the path to that pitiful little hovel you live in. No one wants anything to do with your family, not with the stink of your mother's sins on your skin like old blood." He ran his nose up my neck as if he could smell the shroud of maternal shame passed onto me.

"Please leave me be, Yorick, I have to get home to my mother. She is ailing. I must make her her tea."

His eyes hardened to two silver chips of ice, and in a heart-stuttering yank, he pulled me close enough that the stubbled growth on his chin scraped against my cheek as he pulled me up to his level. My toes grappled for purchase on the slick stones, and I was forced to fist his tunic to keep from falling. My breaths were uneven, sawing their way in and out of my clenched teeth, burning in my chest around the shards of panic stabbing through my lungs.

"That heinous bitch doesn't deserve your attention," His words were viperous, whispered through gnashing teeth and angry spittle that struck my cheek. "But gods damn, Rosewynn, I do."

My scalp burned as he twisted harder, giving me a mind-rattling shake. My bleary eyes darted furtively around the square, hoping to find someone, anyone who would see my panic and come to my aid. But we were utterly and devastatingly alone. I pressed my lips into a thin line, refusing to give him the satisfaction of crying out even as he cast me to the ground, my head cracking against the lip of the well.

Bells filled my ears, chiming in unison in one long, ringing note. My vision kaleidoscoped, twisting and multiplying the man before me as he bent to brandish an accusatory finger in my face. "I will have you one day,

Rosewynn. She'll be dead, and you'll be mine."

The blood on the back of my head was tacky as I made my way home. The widow Gershwynn woke me from where I lay half frozen at the base of the well in my own blood with the toe of her boot kicked squarely into my ribs. She spat at my feet as I struggled, palms slipping against the snow and the ice pink from my head wound. "You're no better than that miserable trollop who spawned you, girl, with all that innocent blood on her hands.

They should have left her where they found her." I staggered to my feet, gathered my half-full frozen bucket of water, and began to limp back out of town even as the widow admonished me, condemning me for my pitiless existence with her arthritic fingers, until I could no longer hear her acrid words.

My head felt leaden, and my vision spiraled as I threaded my way through trees and back onto the path homeward. I should have stopped by the physicians on the way, but we had no more for doctors' cures. A root grabbed me by the ankle and pulled me down into the sinking slushed-up trail.

"Oi, are you drunk?" a man's voice, lilting and annoyed, said from the recessed shadows of the trees behind.

Hands reached out and scooped me under my arms and helped to set me back on my feet. "You ought to watch . . . oh, it's you." I turned to thank whoever had helped me to find the Larkins' eldest son, his kind face crumpled in disgust as he set his eyes upon me.

"It's me." I laughed, but it was hollow and mirthless as he began to scrub the taint of touching me from his palms against the wool of his fine coat.

He grumbled obscenities under his breath and shoved past me, nearly knocking me off my feet yet again, without so much as a goodbye or a glance over his shoulder. I trudged on, imagining him ducking into a warm home gilded in golden firelight to tell his family and his pretty, plump fiancée about his near brush with the pariah Rosewynn. Their mouths would form prim little O's as they gasped in horror and ran to fetch a pitcher of warmed water and soap so he could scrub the scourge that was her off his skin lest the single act of kindness curse their family as my mother's presence had supposedly cursed so many others and brought them to their bloody and untimely dooms.

The fire in the hearth was in its death throes by the time I slid through the door. "You're bleeding," my mother croaked from where she knelt beside the hearth like a loved one next to a funerary bed. Curse her and her keen eyes, unafflicted by age and illness like all her other bodily senses.

"It's nothing. I was careless on the ice is all." I slung the water pail up onto the counter and began to fill our weary kettle with dried herbs muddled together in a mortar and pestle. Mullin and ivy for her cough, skullcap and catmint for the inflammation in her withering lungs. They smelled dusty and aged, long past their prime potency, but the winter had been long, and our stores had to be stretched.

"You're never carless." Her words seethed with suspicion and were pasted with phlegm.

I took the kettle to the hook by the hearth and set it over the pitiable excuse of a fire all the while avoiding her eyes that glinted, gilded by the aureate ember light. "Well, today I was." I helped her back into her chair and tucked the once-heavy blanket, now worn through with holes made by the mouths of moths, around her legs. Our wood box was full of pithy, pulpy pine that burned as quick as paper, but I fed the hearth, and it devoured the offering eagerly and set the tea to a steady screaming boil in no time at all while I sat at my mother's feet and allowed her to absently pluck the petals from my blood-matted hair with her feeble, trembling fingers. I poured her a mug, and with a pang between my ribs, I wished there was honey left in the jar to make the skunky concoction more palatable. But the bees had long since died after the frost failed to lift even as the seasons should have changed.

Raking my fingers through my hair to loosen the last strands that still clung to the idea of being in a braid, and I stilled. My ribbon, the one that had fixed the flowers to the fence, was gone.

"My ribbon," I murmured, as I handed my mother her steaming mug. "Did you see my ribbon?"

Her brow furrowed as she blew the tempest from the lip of her cup. "You must have lost it. There was nothing but bruised petals and matted blood in your hair, dear."

My stomach tied itself into knots and bows that twisted and tangled. The slip of green must have been snatched along my route home by a gnarled and bare branch envious of the scrap of color. Perhaps if fortune was with me, I would find it again on my next venture into town.

"Good night, Mother." I kissed her crown, but I knew it did not carry the weight and warmth of the dutiful, loving daughter I played at being, just as her maternal ministrations earlier had been nothing but the echo of what once was. Duty and grief had long since masticated and gobbled up whatever familial fondness we'd had for one another when we put my father in his grave.

That night, and for several nights after, despite my mother's warnings, I slipped over the sill of my window and lingered in the garden until the night sky bled into dawn, inexplicably hoping to see a flash of amber eyes in the suffocating darkness. But sleep always took me before there was anything to see except for frost-burned withering plants and the ghosts of my footsteps on the frozen ground. But each morning when I awoke, there was a fresh bouquet of beasts-bane lying on the icy snow like a broken bird laid in offering by a feisty feline at its owner's feet.

One eve as the fiery shades of autumn bled out of the world only to be replaced by the blue hues of winter, the woman who would become the moon sat on the stoop of their home darning in the fading golden light when her father came home. On his heels like a second shadow drawn thin in the waning of the sun was a man to whom her father had determined she should wed. The man had crooked and yellowed teeth, and his fingers were lank and long where they bunched on the crumpled rim of his hat. His eyes were damp, leering, and lecherous, and he made the woman feel all together uneasy in a way that made her want to pull a veil over her eyes and hide from his gaze.

"He has gold," her father said.

"He has a home with plenty of rooms for children," her mother said.

But the woman cared not for his gold nor to have her belly grow thick with his long-fingered, dewy-eyed spawn. She longed for a simple life with the woodsman whom she loved, with his kind amber eyes and gentle steadying presence. And so in the dark of the night, together they ran away.

But fortune was not on the young couple's side.

The next morning, the bells rang at the church to summon the bride to meet at the altar her bridegroom. With each passing moment that the long-fingered man stood waiting, venom spilled into his veins, the sort born of a green-eyed snake that hisses and whispers vile with its fangs sunk deep into hateful hearts. Until in the name of vengeance to retrieve his bride he claimed stolen, he took up an axe and took to the woods to hunt.

The gentle tap of moonlight stroking my cheek through the parting clouds on a wisp of wind roused me from my slumber. For a moment, with the cold spidered across my bones and the dark behind my lids, I thought perhaps I lay in the soil adjacent to the worm-eaten decomposed remains of my father. But then in a flutter of snow flurries and eyelashes, I looked out upon the world and found twin amber eyes peering at me from inches away through the bars of the fence upon which I leaned.

"You're here." If it weren't for the puff of breath the words traced in the air, I might have thought I was dreaming still.

"I'm always here, Little Wolf." The beast's lips curled into half of a smile that showed me the tiniest hint of his elongated canines. "I brought these for you again."

The soft brush of flower petals, like butterfly kisses made with eyelashes, brushed against my fingers where my hand lay in my lap, I stroked the ruffled edge of one of the bells reverently and imagined for a moment that his lips might feel just as soft under my touch. "Why do you always leave them for me?"

His eyes sparked like a pitch filled fire as they met mine. "Because they make you smile."

I could taste his words. He spoke them so close to me I wanted to wrap them around my tongue and savor every syllable like sweet nectar.

"How do you know that? You're never here when I find them." The iron bit into my cheek as I pressed my face closer to his through the bars. Our noses brushed, and that touch alone was nearly rapturous. When had my heart become so endeared to this monster?

His eyebrow quirked. "Am I not?" If I breathed too deeply, our mouths would collide in a cataclysmic kiss that impossibly and ridiculously felt worth dying for, for if I was seen by anyone, even my own mother, consorting with such a creature, they would consider me in his thrall and string me up as readily as they strung up feast day decorations.

The sounds of hinges squealing sent me skittering like a rabbit into the ratty brush of our winter garden. "Rosewynn?" My mother's voice cracked like thawing river ice. "Rosewynn, where are you?"

She stumbled out into the snow, and her shawl slipped off one shoulder, little more than a bony prominence now that sickness and ill eating had sapped her of her fatted health. With a flashed glance to make certain of the beast's retreat, I rose from my crouched place and cleared my throat, the flowers tucked into the crooked space between elbow and rib below my cloak. "I'm here, Mother."

Her eyes found me, despite the silver and blue hues of the dark. "What did I tell you about being out at night? Get back in here."

My heartstrings pulled, treading back through my ribs and spine to where they tangled around the bars of the fence, and reached beyond, reached for him. With every step away, they ached, but I gave in, as I always did, to my mother's demands and accompanied her indoors.

Wrinkled potatoes, more shriveled than the face of the aged man who'd sold them to me, filled my basket along with a bunch of pitiable onions and a head of browning cabbage. My rumbling stomach had hoped to find some soup bones at the market, but they were far and few between. The stews in the days ahead would be thin, but we would make do, we always did.

I dawdled on the way home, pausing every time the sun's watery rays managed to slice through the curtain of clouds to let it warm my hunger-hollowed cheeks. It wasn't happiness that I felt, but something not dissimilar from it when the sun kissed my eyelashes. It reminded me of better days before the man I'd called my father died, back when my mother sang and the garden thrived, before the long winter descended, and empty bellies made for bitter neighbors—who, if I were honest, weren't particularly friendly to begin with. Those memories were faded and frayed from being pulled out and tucked away in my mind over and over again.

On our stoop, I did my best to kick the frozen mud from my boots before heading inside. As soon as I turned the knob and pushed the door in, I wished I'd done anything else. Kept walking until I hit the farthest corner of the fence. I could've climbed it and kept going into the woods until I found a pair of gleaming golden eyes or until some creature turned me into its supper, my sinew stuck in its teeth. Anything would have been better than opening that front door to find my mother and Yorick sitting amiably at the table, a red betrothal cloak between them.

The sun stabbed through our threadbare curtains to illuminate the spot it sat almost as if to mock me and the near joy I'd felt only a heartbeat before. My mother stood, her sallow face split into a shaky smile, and said, "Darling, there you are." Her hands trembled as she soothed them over her ratty apron. "We've been waiting."

My throat worked on the swollen, sour lump of dread lodged in it. I couldn't seem to tear my eyes off the brilliant scarlet wool, its edges embroidered with stark white flowers. "What is this?" My words were raspy and far less sturdy than I wished them to be.

Yorick stood and crossed the small space to loom in front of me in two quick strides. I flinched as he grabbed the handle of my basket, his voice thick with falsely honeyed sentiment as he said, "Let me take that for you, Rosewynn, come sit with your mother and me. We have much to discuss." My eyes went wide as I noted the blood-stained length of green silk wound around his wrist, my ribbon. The brute wore it like a damn trophy.

I did as I was bidden, though I shook my head, my hair tumbling from its knot, in disbelief, not quite sure that I hadn't slipped into an actual nightmare. My mother spoke, but the words didn't make sense. I couldn't focus on them, not when Yorick sat opposite looking at me with his lips curled in a wicked and indolent smirk.

Certain words and phrases stuck like barbs: marriage, security, no other options, not getting better, a good man.

My mother stood, gathering my normal gray cloak in her swollen-knuckled fingers, with murmured words about allowing the two of us a moment to speak alone, before tossing it into the fire where the flames greedily ate each fiber.

As soon as she'd drifted like a wraith from the room, Yorick shoved the carmine-colored cloak across the table at me, a grim laugh on his lips. I looked up, defiantly meeting his predacious gaze.

"I told you, you'd be mine," he said. He rapped his knuckles on the table before standing and sauntering to leave my home. I should have left it at that, should have let him leave. It seemed it was to be a day full of wrong choices and regrets.

"I'd like my ribbon back," I said with more steel and spine than I knew I should when speaking to him. I saw it in the way the words struck his back. His shoulders went rigid, and his fist at his side clenched so hard the skin turned pale.

He was above me in a preternatural instant. His face leered, but his eyes, oh gods his eyes had darkened. They'd honed into twin lethal points, like the heads of arrows aimed straight at my heart. "This old thing?" He unspooled it from his wrist with jerked and precise movements.

"Yes," I said through gritted teeth, but the hiss of the s on the end of the word was strangled as he wrapped the cord of silk around my throat and twisted it. I'd seen farmers garrote their hogs before market days, and I imagined that this swift pressure, this theft of air and kicking of feet was not too dissimilar to what it felt to be one of those swine as they looked their slaughterers in their eyes. But I had one thing they didn't, the surety that Yorick wanted my body for more than just a fine meal to sup upon.

"I'll have to teach you some better manners, betrothed." His face dotted over with black, and then with a slip of his long fingers, he released me, taking my ribbon with him. Breath rushed into my lungs in a torrent. "You can have it back on our wedding day, my dear," my husband-to-be hissed in my ear, before he licked the salt of my tears from my cheek in one long, languid stroke that made my viscera curdle. And then with the slam of a door, he was gone.

A shrill sob clawed its way into my throat and roosted there as I shouted, "Mother!"

I shoved off the chair so fast it skidded back into the wall and fractured, its snap ricocheting around the room as loud as a tree felled in an otherwise silent forest, but I didn't care.

My mother bled like a shadow from my room where she'd hidden herself, wringing her arthritic fingers against her ribs like the flapping of a dying dove. "It—it's for your own good."

"How in the gods names is marrying that beast of a man for my own blessed good?" I wished so desperately for the tears to stop falling, for the thin line of pain that encircled my neck, red and angry and raw, to stop burning, but neither wish came true.

"Because it's all true, every nasty black mark and rumor that besmirches my name is true!" Her words tore at the edges, shredded over her teeth, and the anguish in them stilled me.

How could it all be true? All the deaths pinned to her, all the blame?

Mother stumbled her way to her rocking chair in the flicker of the firelight and put her head in her hands. "I am what they say, a woman born of witches and beasts, from beyond the wall. I murdered those who took me in when they discovered my secret, when I couldn't hide it anymore, before I learned how to control it. I ensorcelled my husband into marrying me, and when he found out, when the spell at last grew thin, when I could no longer pay its price, he hanged himself."

Disbelief wrapped its ugly hand around my heart and squeezed.

"What do you mean . . . no, that's not right, he died—"

"By his own hand. I lied to you," my mother interrupted.

"No. No, he wouldn't do that to me, he loved . . ." Realization dawned like the bloom of pain from a knife thrown at a back, striking true. "You called him your husband, but you never said—"

"That he was your father. No. I didn't." She held my eyes resolvedly for what felt like an achingly tense moment fraught with so many unspoken and unnamable emotions. "I was pregnant when the Huntsmen found me in the woods. They saw a beast on me, its teeth upon my flesh, and they killed it without question. Some of them wanted to leave me there, I wasn't of their village, you know the rules. But they voted and decided to bring me back with them. They assumed I'd been lost off one of the trader's caravans, and I never said a word to discount that belief."

"So I am . . ." My eyes flicked to my door, to where the window lay waiting for me to fling it open and go to the beast who'd been lurking outside the warded fence.

"You are born of bestial blood, but the magic I worked upon you at birth and the aspects of your witch nature will suppress that part of you."

"For how long?" I hissed, aware that anger brewed in every spat syllable.

She shrugged the nubs of her shoulders that jutted through her threadbare shawl like the prominences of bats' wings. "I don't know. It could be triggered by spending too much time near the wilder wood, or it could lie within you sleeping until you die."

"You had no right!" I yelled, unable to tether the anger I felt to my ribs to keep it from flying loose and wreaking havoc.

Her eyes watered—not with tears, but with deep apathy. "I had every right. I'm your mother."

I sat on my bed waiting for the moon to rise, watching the frost spindle across the windowpanes like the silk of a busy spider. The cloak hung like a death sentence from the finial on the bedpost. Weddings always took place on the new moon; it was then that all beasts supposedly slept, which was why it was deemed the most auspicious in the lunar cycle for people to wed. It was believed that a peaceful moon meant a peaceful marriage, but I knew mine would be anything but.

With a sigh, I stood and slung the cloak over my shoulders. The fabric was stiff with newness, but it was much warmer than the cloak my mother had burned. Still, I loathed the places it touched my skin; it felt like his lecherous hands on me.

The window rasped, gritting its teeth against the breath of frozen air that rushed in as I threw it open and slipped over the sill. The snow crunched softly beneath my feet like the fragmented remains of broken hearts going to their deaths with a whisper rather than a scream.

A tide of fog rolled in, cascading out of the densely packed woods beyond the fence until it was so thick I had to wade in it as I walked from shrub to shrub plucking winter berries to fill my pockets as I went. I dusted the downy layer of snow from the glass tops of the garden's few cold frames to peer at the incubating fist-sized squash within.

I felt him arrive, those eyes a tingling brand upon my back as tangible as a caress, before I turned around. He leaned against the iron that was meant to repel him as casually as if he'd been there all this time waiting for me.

There was a ruby droplet of blood below his smirking lip. A fire stoked in my belly from embers I'd thought long dead, as I was suddenly struck with the decidedly reckless urge to suck it off his lip. As if he could read my darkest impulses, his lips curled into a broader smile. "Miss me, Little Wolf?"

I crossed my arms over my chest; my heart was hammering against my ribs with such fervor it was as though it thought to escape and serve itself to the beast on a silver platter. "I should say not." I needed this, needed to bandy salacious words with him after the day I'd had. It was a balm to my singed and cinder heart.

"Liar." His eyes flashed with what may have been mirth, or perhaps he was just ravenous and looking for dessert. "New cloak?"

I edged closer, inexorably drawn to him by an inexplicable thread of desire and trepidation so thick and palpable I could almost see it connecting us, pearlescent in the mist.

I wrapped my fingers around the bars, their icy burn biting through my gloves. "You have blood on your face, Beast." I had to tilt my chin up to see him fully at this angle, exposing the long column of my pale neck, the vulnerable blue veins throbbing just below the surface.

He ran his thumb across the underside of his mouth and then sucked the pretty red droplet from its pad. "Apologies. I had a late supper." His eyes locked unblinkingly on mine, the corners of which crinkled with mischief.

"Anyone I know?" I teased, but the words were hitched and breathy—part humor, part hesitation. After all, who in their right mind teased a monster? Another monster I supposed, so then it only made sense.

His smile was feral, all white fangs and devious notions. "Why? Did you have someone in mind?" But then his brows furrowed, drawn together by a single stitch of concern. "Mayhap the one who gave you that betrothal cloak?" He reached between us to twist his clawlike fingers around the crimson ties of my cloak as if he were toying with the idea of ripping them open.

My thoughts stumbled. "How . . ."

He snipped my words off with sharper ones of his own. "I know many things, Little Wolf." He bowed his head, his breath hot and hovering over my pulse, so close I felt his next words whispered like a promise against my skin. "Meet me, the night of the full moon, Little Wolf. We'll take care of your . . . problems."

When I opened my eyes, he'd disappeared like a dying breath on the wind.

The woodsman the woman sought to marry had many brothers, and it was one such of these that saw Long-fingers leaving the church with an axe in his hand and murder in his eyes. The woodsman ran on sure feet through the brush and brambles that would trip ordinary men, but he and all the others in his family were no ordinary men. They were men of the forest with sap on their fingers and twigs in their hair. They were men who knew each in breath and out breath of the trees, and so he made it to their family home in time to warn his brother and his pale love that Long-fingers was coming.

The woman who was to become the moon begged her woodsman to run with her, to go to a faraway place where none could reach them. But instead, it was decided after much hastened discussion that they would go instead to the witch who lived in the heart of the woods and seek her council.

The warp and weft of this woven tale here grows thin, for it is unclear what happened in the darkest depths of the wood on that day, but what is known is thus:

The woman fell upon the witch's threshold alone, the blood of her love sullying her pale complexion. The shred of her skirts appeared decidedly axe-bladed in shape, and she scrambled to her knees and begged the witch to send her where no mortal man could touch her again so she might never know the bonds of a marriage to the long-fingered man nor any other of his ilk.

With careful consideration, the witch acquiesced, for she too had once suffered the fate of a broken heart, but that is an altogether different story. And taking pity on her, the crone sent her to her lonely perch in the sky. But the moon who was once a woman was gone, was still hunted, and it was not long after that the long-fingered man came to rest on the front stair of the witch's porch and demanded she preform magics for him.

And so it is said that for an unknown price, the witch cursed the pack of the woodsman's kin to bestial forms, forever haunted by the death of their brother, forever hungry for their revenge on the long-fingered man and any descended from him.

Light spilled opalescent across the ivory snowscape, illuminating the path to the fence where he already waited, like the aisle of a bride.

The moon hung swollen in the sky, burgeoning with crystalline brilliance. It skimmed the treetops, as though its full weight was difficult to drag to its zenith. It kept pausing to rest, swathing itself in the crushed velvet of the night.

I hovered under the eaves' overhang, lingering in the shadows. But he saw me. His gaze crashed into mine with a cataclysmic force that made my knees tremble.

"Are you going to come out and play, Little Wolf?" he snarled, his words sent on the wind to wrap around my heart and pull me forward. I was at the bars in an instant.

He nosed the side of my neck, one hand slipping beneath my cloak to hook my hip and pull me closer, our bodies pressed painfully against the iron, but I didn't want to pull back, and it seemed neither did he. My breaths heaved against my bosom as his lips met mine with a feverish fervor. He tasted crisp like the smell of pine on a winter wind; he tasted like the freedom I craved nearly as much as I craved this kiss.

I moaned when he pulled back, his golden eyes flashing feral as he snagged my gaze. "Tell me, Little Wolf, do you want to be let loose from your cage?"

My heart fluttered as delicate hope, fragile and new like the wings of a freshly hatched butterfly, brushed against it. "Yes." The single word floated breathily between us.

His gaze darkened, and his lips curled, exposing a slender fang as lethal as any dagger, but the thrill that raced along my bones at the look in his eyes, his pupils blown wide, suppressed any alarm that I might have felt.

His hands bunched in the dowdy fabric of my dress below my laced bodice. "Lift your skirts, Little Wolf."

The words fell from his lips mesmeric, heady, and dark; they brokered no argument, no question or hesitation. For a breath, there was no sound in all the world aside from the rustle of cloth as I pulled it up inch by inch, exposing the milky length of my legs to him.

"Hold on to the bars tightly, Rosewynn," he growled. The words slipped under my skin and thundered through my veins to run rampant as he fisted the bunched wool.

I obeyed, wrapping my gloved fingers round them until I could feel my knuckles go white, the sting of cold nipping at my palms through the knit threads pulled taut. He sank to his knees before me. One hand caressed my leg from ankle to the apex of my thighs, pulling a gasp from me. He scooped up my thigh, dragged it between two bars, and settled it over his shoulder like a hunter with his kill.

He bent his head as if in worship and wrote rapturous poetry with his tongue across the soft, wet, and delicate parts of me.

I began to unravel, a string from my molten core pulled until I felt as though I might come apart. I threw my head back, moaning from deep within my soul as he unmade me with every swirl of his tongue. I locked eyes with the silver moon as she spied on us from her trek through the sky and thanked her for bringing me my monster.

Fingers replaced tongue as he stood, and he pressed kisses like starlight along the tipped column of my neck until he found the path to my earlobe that he gently pinched between his fang and lip. Huskily, he whispered, "Come for me, Little Wolf."

So, I did. I let myself fall to pieces. I was beautifully broken, like a shooting star burning brightly before crashing from the heavens into the mortal plane. For a bliss-ridden moment, I was shimmering luminescent destruction, and then I was myself again, all quavering limbs and pleasant aches.

"I love watching you come undone." The beast's words scratched against my ear. "I don't know that there will ever be enough of that for me in this lifetime."

I laughed, satiated, against his chest, the nip of an iron bar crisp against my cheek, listening to his heartbeat run wild, to the words rumble through him a moment before they were uttered aloud as his fingers knotted in my windswept hair. "I'm sorry for this next part, Rosewynn, it's going to hurt."

Fear only had a moment to sluice through me before pain-fueled rigor gripped me in its fist as twin fangs sank deep into that tender place where my neck met my shoulder. My mouth contorted in a silent scream. The moon winced and turned her head from me as the edges of my vision bled black.

A cold hand stroked my cheek. No, not a hand, it was the hard and unyielding press of rusty, frozen ground. I fluttered freshly fallen snowflakes from my eyelashes, only to find mischievous golden eyes staring at my face intently from between the bars. I couldn't tell if the metallic tang in the air was from the rusty iron or my spilled blood, but either way, the air I breathed was thick with it. It coated the back of my throat, scratching it until I coughed.

My rasp became a snarl, the sound starting low in my throat before sawing its way free. "You bit me." My words sounded peculiar, not quite my own, slightly slurred. I pressed fingers to my lips. My teeth were larger, longer, lethal.

A wry twist curled on the edge of the beast's unnervingly handsome and wicked mouth. "Show me your teeth, Little Wolf." His words were steeped in devious mirth. He'd known, known the whole time about that secret part of me that my mother had tried to suppress.

I looked down at my hands, realization lit in my mind and coaxed alive slowly. Their ends were twisted into talons that had a deadly razor-like shine against the stark white innocence of the snow. He'd asked if I'd wanted freedom, and I'd naively said yes without question. I'd assumed he'd break the rust-weakened bars to let me from my cage, but never had I fathomed this.

He'd unmade and remade me into something new, something stronger, something I was always meant to be. It was glorious.

I pushed myself to sitting, brushing errant strands of hair from my face, so I was nearly eye level with where he crouched. "Listen close, Little Wolf, the witch's enchantment on these bars prevents them from being broken no matter how corrupted they are by time. It also prevents the gate from being opened from the outside; only someone on the inside can do that." He reached through the bars to cup my cheek. "Only you can set yourself free."

My new fangs nipped my swollen bottom lip as a smile spread across my face. "I understand."

His lips crashed into mine with a savage, bruising passion that sparked and crackled along my skin. It knotted us together body and soul, each of us claiming the other, branding one another as something more than lovers, something more than beasts. When he pulled back, he took a piece of me with him. "I'll meet you beyond the iron gate." His words promised a life, a full life together, as we both stood, and he vanished with preternatural speed into the dark of the wood.

The guilt at leaving my mother lodged itself like a knife in my gut, bleeding spite and nausea into my belly. Ours was not a relationship born out of love, but of duty, and yet I found I could not take a single step on the path toward the town without seeing her one last time. I opened the back door and crept across the crooked threshold, only to be wrapped in a suffocating silence, and in a single heartbeat, I knew that death had come to whisk her away to that place of eternal rest at last.

Her papery white skin was waxy in the light of the dying embers, her jaw hung slack, her eyes closed. I didn't feel sadness like I had when the man who had been my father passed. Instead, I felt something lighter, more hopeful. And the bitter ill feelings of guilt eased along with it; at least I was not leaving her alone, for she'd already left.

I kissed her forehead before grabbing the flint upon the hearth. With a few hard strikes, I caught the thatch of our roof alight before I strode out the front door, leaving my old life to burn behind me.

The ice on the wind stung my cheeks as I ran through the woods, unencumbered by the human need to watch my step. My red cloak streamed behind me, like blood rippling on water, in a breeze. My senses were as sharp as jagged glass. I could hear people's breaths as they slumbered in their homes. I could smell their sweat, their nightmares.

The square unfolded before me, vacant save for a single Huntsman on guard, barely a shadow where he leaned against the gate. I knew without question who it was that bared my way, the smell of his brutish conceit unmistakable.

I prowled forward, the breeze twisting around my skirts, toying with their ragged hems as it chased snowflakes across the stones. My footsteps echoed across the hollow darkness between me and Yorick. I saw his shoulders stiffen and his brows knit in anger as he stepped forward into a pale shaft of moonlight.

He opened his mouth to speak, but the only sound that came out was a sickly wet sort of squelch as I descended on him, all fangs and claws and brutal vengeance.

Fear flooded his eyes as I brought him to his knees, my talons wrapped around his jaw. I glared down at him pouring every ounce of loathing I had for him into my stare as I bent, and hissed, "I will never be yours." With the crack of his neck, I blew out the light in his eyes as easily as if it were a flame dancing upon a candlewick.

I pulled my ribbon from his wrist and tied my windswept hair back before I gleefully painted the square with his blood in broad strokes, hanging his innards like holiday garlands across the fence before I opened the gate to find my yellow-eyed beast waiting for me with an outstretched hand.

My first step beyond the gate filled my lungs with unrestrained joy, I twined my fingers with the beast's, letting him pull me close, the bond between us humming with the vibrancy and intensity of a lightning strike as he bent to kiss me. His hand caressed my face, leaving streaks in the gore that painted my cheeks scarlet. He pulled away reluctantly with a growl as a scream sliced through the silence.

We turned to see the widow Gershwynn by the well, pointing a damning finger at the pair of us, our bodies pressed together, her mouth in a perfect O before she collapsed in a heap of shock and ill-fed bones on the cobbled stones.

He whispered against my blood-matted hair, "Let's go home."

I answered with a nod.

Our hands locked together, we ran on deft feet into the dense woods. The full-bellied moon followed our every step with bold curiosity, painting the snow on the ground with a silver glow through the dappled branches. Together, we howled unrestrained into the crisp night air, the song coming from that place deep within me that the beast had awakened.

I was a wolf after all. Another monster in the dark.

M.A. Brown is a stay-at-home-schooling mom living in Colorado with her husband and four kids. She loves to write fantasy with a healthy dose of romance, dreamy worlds, and a whole lot of magic. When she's not creating, she enjoys hiking, camping, and gardening with her family.

Follow her @writer.m.a.brown or find her on her website www.mabrownauthor.com.

BEYOND THE IRON GATE

R eaders, Thank you for reading and taking a chance on my words.

This story was originally intended as a submission for an anthology, but in a fit of imposter syndrome I decided not to turn it in at the last minute. It was one of the best decisions I've made though I admittedly made it for the wrong reasons. But from this one story The Pennies Worth of Dread novella series came to be, and I can't wait to share more dark weird seasonally inspired little romances with you all.

To everyone that helped this story come into being, to my husband who made a little red riding hood joke that inspired this story, to Nina who read the very first crusty draft over a year ago, to Beth Steadman who helped me expand the tale and told me the spice was some of the most unique she'd read, to Cynthia for your incredible support and beta feedback, to Giulia my immensely talented artist who brought my character and cover visions to life, and to Chrissy who edited my words to make them readable... I couldn't have done this without you.

And As always, last but never least, thank you God for giving me the ability to dream up worlds and spill them across a page.

Also by M.A. Brown

The Travelers Series

The Songs That Beckon

Echo Across The Sands

Whispers From The Fade (*Coming Soon*)

A Pennies Worth of Dread

Beyond The Iron Gate

Beneath The Silvern Pond (*Coming Soon*)

The Seventh Sister (*Coming August 6th, 2025*)

I f you enjoyed Beyond the Iron Gate, please consider leaving a review on Goodreads, Amazon or on social media, then check out some more books by Midnight Tide Publishing.

Thank you for reading.

The Big Bad Wolf never killed for fun—he was on a mission.

Niklaus von Brandt is leading a double life. Some days he wields cleavers in his stepfather's butcher shop, and others, he transforms into a lethal instrument—a skilled assassin, prowling the kingdom's darkest corners.

Abendrot was founded by werewolves but is now ruled by humans who have one goal: to eradicate the werewolves. Now, to protect his family, Niklaus must embrace his moniker, the one the kingdom murmurs about—The Big Bad Wolf.

Yet within the opulent halls of the castle lies a secret, and Niklaus plans to use it to his advantage. Even if it means exploiting the eldest princess.

As tensions escalate, and loyalties blur, Niklaus must navigate a treacherous game of power and deception. Where every decision carries the weight of survival—for himself, his family, and the fate of Abendrot itself.

The Hunter series offers a captivating blend of supernatural fantasy romance, brimming with werewolves, assassins, political intrigue, sharp wit, and thrilling battles. Perfect for fans of From Blood and Ash by Jennifer L. Armentrout, My Fair Assassin by C.J. Anaya, A Kiss of Iron by Clare Sager, and Throne of Glass by Sarah J. Maas. Embark on a journey where passion, danger, and secrets collide in a mesmerizing world of magic and mystery.

He's a Vampyr.
I'm a Korama.
And I love him.

Tough-as-nails Verity 'Veri' Eadaoin has never trusted Vampyrs. They've killed everyone she loves. She finally gets an opportunity for revenge after a deadly Vampyr raid against her pack. Her new mission: retaliate against the Vampyr Queen by killing her newly-minted Prince. Simple enough. But Verity is unprepared

for her encounter with the unsus-
pecting Vampyr.

Still reeling from his murder in Sague-
nay, Darren Pierce-Crané is fresh-
ly-turned and reluctant. He's barely
begun to adjust to his unlife when
there's a wolf at his door. Darren
barters for his survival, resulting in a
precarious pact with Verity. This deal
uncovers sinister secrets that could
spell the undoing of the entire city.

War is on the horizon, and time is of
the essence. Verity and Darren will
have to decide what is most impor-
tant to them: their faction or each
other.